Why the Frog Has Big Eyes

Why the Frog Has Big Eyes

Betsy Franco

Illustrated by Joung Un Kim

Green Light Readers
Harcourt, Inc.

Orlando   Austin   New York   San Diego   Toronto   London

Long ago, all frogs had small eyes.

One frog sat and stared all day.

"No one can stare as long as I can,"
Frog bragged.

His friends said, "Let's stop his bragging.
Who can stare as long as Frog can?"

Horse trotted in.
"You will blink first," said Frog.
"I will not!" said Horse.

"See!" shouted Frog. "You did!"

Rabbit hopped in.
Rabbit didn't last long.
He blinked first.

"No one is better than I am!"
bragged Frog.

Fish flopped up.
"Frog will blink first this time!"
said Fish.

Fish stared at Frog.
Frog stared at Fish.
Fish didn't blink.
Frog's eyes got big, *big,* BIG.

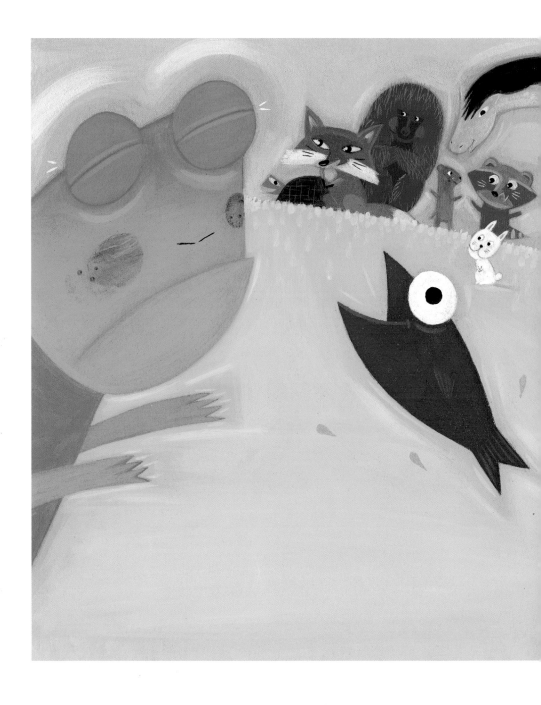

"Frog blinked!" shouted Fish.
"Frog, a fish can't blink! Ha! Ha!"

Frog sat still.
His big eyes stared from that day on.

He didn't brag again.

FROG CHAIN

Make a paper chain that shows how tadpoles become frogs.

WHAT YOU'LL NEED

 paper

 crayons or markers

tape

1. **Think about how tadpoles change into frogs.**

2. **Draw the five changes on paper strips.**

3. **Make the paper strips into a chain. Connect each picture with a blank paper strip.**

4. **Share your frog chain with a friend. Tell about each picture.**

Meet the Illustrator

Joung Un Kim visits bookstores and museums to get ideas for her drawings. She likes to try new things. For the story *Why the Frog Has Big Eyes,* she practiced drawing animals. This is the second animal story she has illustrated.

www.HarcourtBooks.com

First Green Light Readers edition 2000
Green Light Readers is a trademark of Harcourt, Inc., registered in the
United States of America and/or other jurisdictions.

The Library of Congress has cataloged an earlier edition as follows:
Franco, Betsy.
Why the frog has big eyes/Betsy Franco; illustrated by Joung Un Kim.
p. cm.
"Green Light Readers."
Summary: A fable explaining how a staring contest left frogs with large eyes.
[1. Fables. 2. Frogs—Fiction.] I. Kim, Joung Un, ill. II. Title.
PZ8.2.F68Wh   2000
[E]—dc21   99-50805
ISBN 0-15-204874-X
ISBN 0-15-204834-0 (pb)

A C E G H F D B
A C E G H F D B (pb)

Ages 5–7
Grades: K–1
Guided Reading Level: C–D
Reading Recovery Level: 7–8

Green Light Readers
For the reader who's ready to GO!

"A must-have for any family with a beginning reader."—*Boston Sunday Herald*

"You can't go wrong with adding several copies of these terrific books to your beginning-to-read collection."—*School Library Journal*

"A winner for the beginner."—*Booklist*

Five Tips to Help Your Child Become a Great Reader

1. Get involved. Reading aloud to and with your child is just as important as encouraging your child to read independently.

2. Be curious. Ask questions about what your child is reading.

3. Make reading fun. Allow your child to pick books on subjects that interest her or him.

4. Words are everywhere—not just in books. Practice reading signs, packages, and cereal boxes with your child.

5. Set a good example. Make sure your child sees YOU reading.

Why Green Light Readers Is the Best Series for Your New Reader

● Created exclusively for beginning readers by some of the biggest and brightest names in children's books

● Reinforces the reading skills your child is learning in school

● Encourages children to read—and finish—books by themselves

● Offers extra enrichment through fun, age-appropriate activities unique to each story

● Incorporates characteristics of the Reading Recovery program used by educators

● Developed with Harcourt School Publishers and credentialed educational consultants

Daniel's Mystery Egg
Alma Flor Ada/G. Brian Karas

A Bed Full of Cats
Holly Keller

Animals on the Go
Jessica Brett/Richard Cowdrey

The Fox and the Stork
Gerald McDermott

Marco's Run
Wesley Cartier/Reynold Ruffins

Boots for Beth
Alex Moran/Lisa Campbell Ernst

Digger Pig and the Turnip
Caron Lee Cohen/Christopher Denise

Catch Me If You Can!
Bernard Most

Tumbleweed Stew
Susan Stevens Crummel/Janet Stevens

The Very Boastful Kangaroo
Bernard Most

The Chick That Wouldn't Hatch
Claire Daniel/Lisa Campbell Ernst

Farmers Market
Carmen Parks/Edward Martinez

Splash!
Ariane Dewey/Jose Aruego

Shoe Town
Janet Stevens/Susan Stevens Crummel

Get That Pest!
Erin Douglas/Wong Herbert Yee

The Enormous Turnip
Alexei Tolstoy/Scott Goto

Why the Frog Has Big Eyes
Betsy Franco/Joung Un Kim

Where Do Frogs Come From?
Alex Vern

I Wonder
Tana Hoban

The Purple Snerd
Rozanne Lanczak Williams/
Mary GrandPré

Look for more Green Light Readers wherever books are sold!